WELCOME TO

Beast Quest

WITHDRAWN

Collect the special coins in this book.
You will earn one gold coin for
every chapter you read.

1

Once you have finished all the chapters,
find out what to do with your gold coins at
the back of the book.

With special thanks to Tabitha Jones

For Ruby and Lily Cowley

www.beastquest.co.uk

ORCHARD BOOKS

First published in Great Britain in 2016 by The Watts Publishing Group

1 3 5 7 9 10 8 6 4 2

Text © 2016 Beast Quest Limited.
Cover and inside illustrations by Steve Sims
© Beast Quest Limited 2016

Beast Quest is a registered trademark of Beast Quest Limited
Series created by Beast Quest Limited, London

A CIP catalogue record for this book is available from the British Library.

ISBN 978 1 40834 078 3

Printed and bound by CPI Group (UK) Ltd, Croydon, CR0 4YY

MIX
Paper from
responsible sources
FSC® C104740

The paper and board used in this book are made from wood from responsible sources

Orchard Books
An imprint of Hachette Children's Group
Part of The Watts Publishing Group Limited
Carmelite House, 50 Victoria Embankment, London EC4Y 0DZ

An Hachette UK Company
www.hachette.co.uk
www.hachettechildrens.co.uk

TemprA
THE TIME STEALER

BY ADAM BLADE

ORCHARD

CONTENTS

STORY ONE

I fail to see what is so special about that so-called Master of the Beasts. He is a snivelling brat, an upstart on a lucky streak. With a few magic jewels and an enchanted shield, he manages to impress the pathetic subjects of Avantia. But put him against a real enemy and strip away his magic charms, then we'll see.

I admit that – once or twice – he's got the best of me. But not this time.

For I have found a way to even the odds. With my new Beast I will expose Tom for what he truly is – a peasant boy who should have stuck to playing with a wooden sword.

And if he is foolish enough to face me, then he will soon find his luck has run out. He will kneel before me, or he will perish.

Your soon-to-be ruler,

Jezrin

1

TRAINING
INTERRUPTED

Tom leaned over the table, watching the sand flow through the timer. A group of armoured soldiers raced towards him. They had to reach the chalk mark on the cobbles before the sand ran out.

This is going to be close!

"You can do it!" Elenna called from her seat at Tom's side. The palace

courtyard echoed with the clank
of armour, mixed with the steady
rasp of sawing from just outside the
main gate, where Captain Harkman
and his men were making repairs to
the drawbridge. Beyond the racing
soldiers, the towers and ramparts of
King Hugo's palace jutted proudly
into the blue sky.

"Come on!" Tom cried, as the first
runner, a wiry, dark-haired soldier
called Arlen, reached the finish line.
Then Harold skidded over just in time
as the last grains of sand trickled
through. Tom flipped the timer over
and they set off in the other direction.
The remaining soldiers collapsed over
the line. Sully gasped for breath. He
was built like an ox, and had little

love of running. He looked up at Tom, his face streaked with sweat.

"How come you get to sit out?" he wheezed.

Tom grinned. "Someone's got to do the timing," he said. "And, anyway, it wouldn't be a fair race. With my golden leg armour, you'd all be eating my dust."

Sully grunted, flopping down on the ground. Arlen and Harold reached the wall and sprinted back, but they were slowing. The timer ran out before they reached the chalk line.

"At ease, everyone!" said Tom.

"I'll join the next race!" Elenna called. "I'm bored of watching you have all the fun."

Elenna jogged to the start line,

where the other soldiers got to their feet, flexing their muscles or leaning on their knees to catch their breath.

"Giving them a break already?" a hearty voice boomed from behind Tom. Tom turned to see Captain Harkman striding across the courtyard, grinning, his tunic dark with sweat. Harkman crossed to Tom's bench and sat down heavily, grabbing a clay water flagon from the table and taking a long drink.

"It's going to be a scorcher!" he said.

Tom nodded. "Two more races, and I'll call it a day. I don't want anyone getting heat stroke."

"Good plan!" Harkman said, then heaved himself back up. "No rest for the wicked!" He took another slug of water before disappearing back through the courtyard gates.

"On your marks!" Tom called to the soldiers. They hunkered down, their eyes on the wall. "Go!" Tom flipped the timer on the table. Elenna shot forwards – alone. No one else moved. "Come on!" Tom shouted. "Elenna doesn't need a head start!" Still no one moved a muscle.

Elenna slowed and turned to the line of soldiers on the starting line. She put her hands on her hips.

"All right," she said. "You can stop joking now." Still there was no response. Elenna scowled and crossed to Tom. "Did you put them up to this?"

Tom shook his head, glancing at the timer on the table. The sand inside seemed to be stuck. Only a few grains had run through. Tom picked it up and gave it a shake, then tried turning it over, but the sand inside didn't budge.

"That's odd!" Elenna said.

More than odd, Tom thought, shifting his gaze to the soldiers on

the starting line. They were leaning at impossible angles, unblinking – not just still, but frozen. And the courtyard was silent. There was no hammering, no birdsong – not even a breath of wind. Tom felt a prickle of fear run down his spine. *What's going on?*

The shutters to the window in the wizard's tower banged open. Daltec leaned out, as pale and wide-eyed as Elenna. "Come quickly!" he cried.

Tom leapt to his feet, and raced towards the tower. He flung open the door and raced up the spiral stairs, Elenna a step behind.

They burst into Daltec's room. Both Aduro and Daltec looked up from a thick book on the table before them. Few things scared Aduro, but the former wizard's face was as pale as parchment. "What's going on?" Tom asked, holding up the sand-timer.

The sand was actually flowing upwards now! Aduro frowned, his brows pinching together. Daltec beckoned Tom to his side.

"We were filling in yesterday's entry in the Chronicles of Avantia just now," he said, pointing down at the huge, leather-bound book. "But our writing disappeared." He tipped the book towards Tom, and flipped through a hunk of pages. All were blank. When he finally reached a spread filled with Aduro's spidery handwriting, Tom recognised the word "Slivka" – a Beast he'd defeated on a recent Quest. But as Tom watched, the words on the page unravelled like a loose strand of wool pulled tight, then disappeared.

"What does it mean?" Elenna asked.

Aduro took a long breath before answering. "I could be wrong," he said, "but this looks like the work of Tempra the Time Stealer – an ancient Beast who can travel through time, feasting on souls."

Tom felt a sudden lurch of dizziness. He blinked and tried to focus on Aduro's face, but the room and everything in it was shimmering, like a reflection in water. A rushing sound filled his ears. Elenna gasped and leant on the table, her eyes tight shut.

Tom concentrated on Aduro's keen, grey eyes, fighting the sickness rising inside him. "So how do we fight this

Beast?" he asked.

"We don't have long," Aduro said. He hurried to a cabinet on the wall and threw it open, making the bottles inside rattle. "The only way we can protect ourselves is by drinking a potion made from Tempra's blood. Here!" He snatched a vial from the cabinet, and pressed it into Tom's hand.

Inside, Tom could see a liquid, so dark a red it was almost black. He uncorked the vial. "Drink this!" he told Elenna, putting the vial to her lips. Elenna gulped down a small mouthful. Tom took a swig, wincing at the bitterness, and held it out to Daltec.

But the wizard dropped it, and the vial shattered, a pool of liquid seeping between the worn floorboards. The

young wizard's face seemed to dissolve,
the colours and lines swirling together.
Everything in the room twisted and
smeared. Elenna let out a cry, and Tom
reached out to steady himself, but the
floor beneath him lurched, pitching
him forwards into blackness.

2

ERRINEL

"Wake up, you lazy brat!"

A harsh female voice spoke into the darkness. Tom's body felt as cold and heavy as clay. He tried to open his eyes but his lids were crusted together. Panic welled inside him. Then the sharp pain of icy water hitting his face jerked him awake.

"Hey!" Tom sat up, shaking droplets from his hair. Faint shafts of sunlight streamed through chinks between wooden boards above him, making bright lines on the dirt floor. The sour smell of musty hay and mouse droppings filled the air. A pale-haired woman glared down at him, holding an empty bucket. Tom gasped as he

recognised her. *Aunt Maria!* But her usually friendly face now looked harsh.

"Don't just sit there gawping!" she snapped. "Get your lazy backside to the forge. Your uncle's been slaving since before dawn. If you two miss today's quota of swords, there'll be all kinds of trouble."

Tom's tongue felt thick and heavy. His temples throbbed. He swallowed, trying to shift the sour taste in his mouth. "How did I get here?" he croaked. "I was at the palace..." He couldn't quite remember what he'd been doing there. Something to do with timers and sand?

His aunt laughed bitterly. "The palace indeed," she said. "You should thank your lucky stars your uncle and

I have kept you safe from there. You've been dreaming. Now, get a move on, or we'll all end up in the palace dungeons!" She turned and pushed through a door, letting a flare of sunlight into the room before the door banged shut.

Tom rubbed his eyes and stared about. He recognised his uncle's barn, but nothing was where it should have been. Dust covered every surface, and the floor was strewn with rusted tools. *Am I dreaming?* he wondered. But it didn't feel like a dream. He eased himself slowly to his feet, to find they were bare and caked with mud. *Where are my boots?* He was dressed in a tunic the colour of dirt, frayed and thin with wear. His wrist, poking from the threadbare sleeve, looked pale and shockingly thin. Tom's stomach twisted suddenly with a fierce hunger pang, a wave of dizziness sweeping over him at the same time.

Fragments of memories flitted through his mind – Aduro's worried face, Elenna bent over a blank white page, a bitter potion as red as blood. And through it all, the sands of an sand-timer ... running upwards.

Tom shook away the broken images, and pushed through the barn door into sunlight. A cool breeze met him, stirring his wet hair. It brought with it the stink of sewage mingled with stale cooking and smoke. As Tom's eyes adjusted, he found himself in a dirt street lined with houses. A little way

off, a wooden forge billowed smoke
into a clear blue sky. It was a view
that Tom knew as well as his own
name. He was in Errinel, the village
where he'd grown up. But something
terrible had happened. The street
that Tom remembered had always

been busy with scampering children and talkative neighbours. Bright flowers had bloomed in every garden, and doors stood open to welcome visitors in. Now, though, the street was deserted and filthy. The gardens were choked with weeds. Flaking

paint covered closed doors, and grimy curtains hung in the windows.

Even the chickens pecking at the ground looked scrawny, clumps of mangy feathers clinging to their scabby skin.

Something's gone badly wrong, and I need to fix it.

The regular chime of iron on iron rose from the nearby forge. Tom followed the path from his old home towards it, stepping carefully. Chicken droppings and worse littered the way.

He reached the wide, open doors of the smithy and stepped inside. A fierce wall of heat hit him.

The sight of his uncle bent over an anvil, hammering red-hot sparks from a glowing blade was familiar to Tom

– except that Henry looked far older than he remembered. His hair and beard were much greyer.

As Tom stepped further into the forge, his uncle looked up.

"About time," Henry barked. "Get to work, lad!" He gestured to a dozen blade-shaped moulds scattered in the straw. They were grimy with flecks of black metal. Tom had scrubbed similar moulds many times as a child. But he didn't have time for that now.

"Uncle," he said, "there's something very wrong in the kingdom. I must speak to King Hugo."

Henry lifted the glowing blade from his anvil with a pair of tongs, and lowered it into a water bath. Only once the hissing had stopped did he look up. In the light of the fire, Tom could see deep lines beneath his uncle's eyes that had never been there before.

"What are you blathering about?" Henry asked. "I could name a hundred things wrong with the kingdom, but the ghost of a king that never was isn't going to help you. Prince Hugo was killed on his coronation thirty years ago, as well you know."

Tom felt a stab of pain in his chest. *Hugo's dead?* He took another look at the dingy forge and his aging uncle. Nothing was as it should be. Anything could be true.

"Who is king, then?" Tom asked.

Henry looked at Tom as if he'd grown a pair of horns. "Did you knock your head falling out of bed this morning?"

he said. "Jezrin is, of course."

Tom knew of only one Jezrin – a powerful wizard who called himself "The Judge", and was evil through and through. *How can he be sitting on the throne of Avantia?*

Tom noticed Henry watching him

closely, scowling. "Look, Tom," he said, "if you're angling for a day off, pretending that you're sick or something, you can think again. I'm not having you turning into a workshy good-for-nothing like your father."

Tom took a sharp breath. He could hardly believe what he'd heard. "My father was Master of the Beasts," he said. "The bravest warrior in Avantia."

Henry gawped. "You're being daft now, lad. My brother never did a day's hard graft in his life. He ran off as soon as things got tough, only coming back to leave your worthless hide on my doorstep. Bravest man, my foot." Henry spat. "I hope the rotten coward's starving in a ditch somewhere. It's about what he deserves."

Tom's fists clenched as he remembered the day he saw his father sacrifice his life to save Avantia. He wanted to shout at his uncle not to speak ill of Taladon. But a clear part of his mind held him back. *This isn't the Errinel or the Henry I know,* he told himself. *Something's happened to them. Something to do with Tempra.*

"Stop idling and get to work," Henry snapped, "or we'll all end up as dinner for Jezrin's—" His uncle stopped. The colour drained from his hollow cheeks and he gestured for Tom to stay quiet. The sound of hoofbeats echoed around them, getting rapidly louder.

"Henry!" Aunt Maria appeared in the doorway, her eyes shiny with tears. "The soldiers! They're here!"

A ROYAL TAX

"They're early!" Henry said, frowning at the swords scattered in the straw and counting under his breath. "Eleven blades," Henry muttered, then swallowed hard. Outside, the sound of hoofbeats came to a stop.

"What's going on?" Tom asked, but Henry just wiped his hands on a rag and hurried out of the forge with Maria. Tom followed them to find half a dozen armoured men on horseback blocking the way.

Henry thrust Maria behind him, and bowed his head. Tom gaped up at the soldiers. Even with greying hair and dark stubble cut through with a scar, Tom recognised the lead soldier as Captain Harkman. But from the cool

contempt on Harkman's face, Tom could see the captain didn't know him.

Harkman glared down, his eyes as cold and hard as tempered steel. "We've come for the royal tax!" he said.

"Yes, sir!" Maria said. Her body trembled as she hurried back into the forge. The sight was too much for Tom to bear.

He stood tall before the soldiers. "By what right?" he cried, but his uncle grabbed the back of his tunic and yanked, almost pulling him over.

"Hold your tongue!" Henry growled. Maria scurried past, carrying an armful of swords. She laid them in the dust before Harkman's horse, then stood, hardly appearing to breathe, while the captain studied the pile.

"There are only eleven here!" Harkman bellowed, spittle flying from his lips. "The new quota is fifteen!"

Henry flinched. "My lord, we were not expecting you for another few days," he said. "If you give us just a bit more time—"

"Enough!" Harkman shouted. "No excuses. Every man must pay the tax or face the consequences." He nodded to the soldiers behind him. Two broad men swung from their saddles and stepped forwards.

Henry blocked their path, holding up his hands. "Please! I beg you!" he said. But the men barged roughly past him and seized Maria by the arms. Maria let out breathy sobs as they bundled her onto the back of a horse.

Tom leapt forwards and grabbed a blade from the pile in the dust. He sprang towards his aunt's captors. But before he could reach the soldiers, a hefty kick between the shoulder blades sent him sprawling.

Tom scrambled up to see Captain Harkman dismount and slide his sword from its sheath.

"Come on then, lad," Harkman said, beckoning with his free hand. Tom circled the captain slowly, his sword raised. Sniggers from Harkman's men mingled with the sobs of Tom's aunt.

I'll show them!

Tom glared at Harkman. "I don't want to hurt you, Captain," he said. "But you have to let my aunt go."

Harkman laughed cruelly. "Tie her

up!" he called over his shoulder.

"That's it!" Tom lunged, bringing his blade down in a wide, double-handed arc. The blow should have been unstoppable. But Harkman flicked it aside as if he were swatting a fly. Tom felt the impact jolt along his arm, the sword spinning from his fingers. He clutched his fist to his chest, tears

of fury and pain welling in his eyes. He felt like a novice taking his first beating. *Where are my sword skills?*

Harkman sheathed his sword and leapt back onto his horse. He glowered down at Henry. "Your lad has spirit," Harkman said. "I'll give him that. But you'd best beat some sense into him quick, or I'll be taking him next."

Henry's eyes slid past Harkman to where Maria was weeping uncontrollably. "Please …" Henry said, his voice cracking. "Take me instead. I'll do anything you ask!"

But Harkman stared down at him as if he were a pair of muddy boots that wanted cleaning. "Twenty blades next time," he said, "or you'll be joining her. Away, men!"

The soldiers kicked their horses viciously and wheeled them round, pounding away in a cloud of dust.

Henry ran a few paces after them, then fell to his knees, head in his hands, sobbing. Tom gritted his teeth and stepped to his uncle's side. "Don't worry, Uncle," he said. "They won't get away with this. I'm going after them, and I'll bring Aunt Maria back."

Henry shook his head. "Don't be daft, lad. It's too late for that. You know as well as I do what happens to those taken to the palace."

"What?" Tom asked.

His uncle looked up at him, his eyes filled with pain. "They're fed to … " Then he growled and smashed his fist into the ground. "Would you really have me say it?"

"Uncle, it can't be too late!" Tom said. "There must be a horse in the village. I'll ride to the palace. I won't let them hurt her."

Henry got stiffly to his feet, and sighed. "You're as mad as old Aduro."

Tom felt a twinge of hope. "The Good Wizard?" he said.

Henry lifted an eyebrow. "I've heard him called a lot of things, but never that. Aduro's no wizard. He's just a smelly old hermit who's a few apples short of a bushel."

Tom's hope swelled. Anyone not familiar with a wizard's ways might well mistake Aduro for a mad man. "Where do I find him?" he asked.

Henry started back towards the

forge, hollow-eyed. "He lives in the old orchard, halfway between here and the Forest of Fear. But there's little more than brambles there now. Old Aduro won't thank you for poking about."

Tom was already scanning the grassland around the village. He quickly spotted what he needed. Behind the forge, in a patch of scrubland, a scrawny old nag champed the grass. Tom strode into the forge and unhitched a saddle from the wall.

"Oh, no, you don't," Henry said, blocking his way. "You're not taking Puddle on some fool's errand." Tom pushed past. "Where do you think you're going?" Henry called. "I can't make twenty swords on my own!" But all the fight seemed to have gone out of him when the soldiers took Maria away.

Tom saddled the horse and climbed up. "I'll be back," Tom told his uncle, "but not until I've got Aunt Maria." He kicked the old horse to a trot and clopped away, following the dusty road.

"You're foolish, just like Taladon!" Henry shouted after him. "You're leaving me to the same fate as your aunt!"

His words were cruel, but Tom summoned a memory of Henry as he had been – a strong village elder, filled with wisdom and love. Somewhere, somehow, that man still had to exist. Tom tightened his grip on the reins and kicked his horse to a canter.

If anyone can help me put this horrible mess right, it's Aduro.

4

THE OLD HERMIT

The road carried Tom through fields going to seed, and scrubby patches of grassland, home to huddles of skinny sheep. The slow *clip-clop* of Puddle's hooves filled Tom with frustration, but he daren't risk exhausting the old horse before reaching the palace.

Troubled thoughts swirled in Tom's mind as he rode. He knew that, somehow, King Hugo had been murdered by Jezrin, many years previously. And since then, things had gone badly in Avantia – that much was clear from the dreadful state of Errinel, and the farmland surrounding it. But there was something more. Something so evil, it could turn good, proud people – people like his uncle and Captain Harkman – cruel and hard. Tom thought of his sand-timer flowing backwards, and of black ink vanishing from a white page.

It all comes back to Tempra the Time Stealer, he thought. *Jezrin must somehow control the Beast.* Puddle's step faltered, jerking Tom from his thoughts. The old horse's head hung low with exhaustion. "Don't worry, friend," Tom said, rubbing the mare's bony flank. "We're almost there. Soon we'll find you a juicy apple." Puddle whickered softly and picked up her pace, as if she understood.

Before long, the road ahead looped to the left, skirting a copse of gnarled trees beyond a bramble thicket.

Tom left Puddle grazing at the side of the road, and pushed through the dense bushes. Thorns tugged at his clothes and skin. Once he was through, he found knee-high grass scattered with rotting apples. Ancient trees stood all around him, bent under the weight of unpicked fruit. Their crooked branches trailed almost to the ground. The stench of fermenting apples hung heavy in the air, along with the buzz of wasps.

"Aduro!" Tom called, peering into the mess of branches and weeds.

"Who goes there?" a crabby voice called back.

"A friend," Tom said. "I need to speak to you." He heard the snap of a twig, and a moment later, a hunched figure in a ragged cloak shambled from between the trees. Aduro's keen grey eyes gazed out from beneath a travel-worn hood. Tom stepped forwards, smiling. But then Aduro put back his hood, and Tom froze. His friend's once-white beard was matted and yellow, his skin was grey with dirt. More dirt blackened his curled fingernails, and threadbare stockings poked from the ends of his boots.

"This is *my* orchard," Aduro said,

his voice cracking with disuse. "I'll destroy anyone who tries to enter." The old wizard bared his teeth and lifted his hands. Bright balls of blue energy cracked in his filthy palms.

Tom stepped back, his hands raised. "I mean no harm!" he said. But Aduro hissed like an angry cat, letting the energy balls fly. Tom flinched, but the balls slammed into the ground at the wizard's feet, blasting Aduro into the air in a puff of thick smoke.

Oh, no!

When the smoke cleared, Tom found Aduro lying on his back, a blackened hole smouldering before him. Tom rushed to his side and put out a hand.

Aduro's gnarled grip was surprisingly strong. Tom pulled the wizard to his feet, then waited while he brushed the dust from his filthy robe. Finally, Aduro lifted his eyes to Tom's face, frowning as he peered closely.

"Do I know you?" he asked.

"Yes ..." Tom started, then he faltered. "Well, sort of."

Aduro laughed, a long hearty cackle. "And they call me mad! Explain yourself, boy."

"You knew me once as Avantia's Master of the Beasts," Tom said.

Aduro narrowed his eyes and tugged at his yellowed beard. "Master of the Beasts, eh?" he said. "That's a term I've not heard in twenty years. Avantia's had no Master of the Beasts for a generation – and you, lad, can't be much older than twelve."The old man trailed off, gazing into the distance. Then his sharp eyes snapped back to Tom's face. "Tell me, why are you here?"

Tom shrugged. "Because, in my time, you were my friend – and a powerful wizard. You're the only person that can help me put things back how they should be. Where I come from – or I should say *when* I come from – many things are different. Hugo is king, and Avantia is prosperous. The only reason Jezrin has the throne now is because he somehow used Tempra the Time Stealer to go back in time and murder Prince Hugo."

Aduro nodded, slowly at first,

but soon Tom saw a spark of fire
kindle in the old man's eyes. "That
is possible," Aduro said. "I read of
such a Beast back when I was an
apprentice wizard. And rumour has
it that Jezrin feeds his enemies to a
monster beneath the palace. Perhaps
that Beast is Tempra."

Tom thought of his aunt, captive
inside the palace, and felt cold. He
squared his shoulders. "I'm heading
to the palace," he said. "I intend to
defeat Jezrin and his Beast. Can you
send me there with your magic?"

The fire in Aduro's eyes vanished.
"Alas, as you witnessed," he said, "I
am rather out of practice. I'd be more
likely to turn you into a snail than
transport you to the palace. However,

I can get you into the City. Wait here."

Tom waited, full of anxious hope as Aduro shuffled away. *If he can transport me to the City, my journey is all but done!*

Aduro crossed to a patch of long grass, and lifted two baskets of apples, sending up a cloud of buzzing wasps. He thrust the baskets towards Tom. "Take them!" he said.

Tom frowned in confusion. "Why?"

Aduro smiled. "Your passage into the City – they won't let you in without something to sell. Now, if you'll excuse me, my apples won't pick themselves. Good luck to you!" He turned and retrieved a staff from against a nearby tree, then wandered away, muttering to himself.

Tom sighed, and headed back to the road, using the baskets to push through the brambles. *At least Puddle won't go hungry!*

Suddenly, Aduro's voice called after him. "Young man?" Tom turned to see Aduro gazing at him. "Who is your father?" the wizard asked.

The words "Taladon the Swift" almost fell from Tom's lips, but then he remembered how his uncle had called Taladon a coward. He couldn't bear to hear the same from Aduro.

"I don't know," Tom answered. "He died before I was born."

Aduro nodded. "I'm sorry to hear that," he said. Then he turned away, and was soon lost to view between tangled branches.

1

5

A LESSON IN MANNERS

After her rest and a juicy apple,
Puddle carried Tom steadily towards
the City. A basket of apples hung
either side of the nag's back, with
Tom's sword buried deep inside one.
Wagons and horses, loaded with
vegetables and grain, passed Tom on
the road. The riders kept their heads
down, but Tom could see all were as

hungry and careworn as his uncle.

The sun climbed high, and the sky deepened to the flawless blue of a warm autumn afternoon. Finally, the walls of the City slid into view around a curve in the road, rising darkly from the dust. Pointed towers overlooked grey stone battlements

tipped with iron spikes. Tom's
stomach churned with horror as he
saw pale skulls glinting on top of
several of them. Black flags fluttered
above the walls, each carrying the
image of a sand-timer, and carrion
birds circled the towers.

Soldiers stood to attention either

side of the open city gate. Tom joined a line of carts waiting to enter. As he drew closer to the city walls, his heart drummed against his ribs. *If they find my sword, I'm doomed.*

The last wagon rumbled through the gates ahead of Tom. A hefty guard with pale eyes stepped forwards.

"What's your business here?" the man said.

"I've come to sell apples, sir," Tom answered, keeping his eyes low.

The guard stepped past him and peered into a basket. Puddle rolled her eyes and blew out an anxious breath. Tom rested a calming hand on the horse's neck. The big guard rummaged through the basket with pudgy fingers, and Tom tensed his muscles, ready to run. Finally, the man chose an apple and took a bite, then gestured towards the gate with his thumb.

"Through there," he said, "towards the palace. Join a queue with the rest of the rabble."

Tom let out his breath. He tapped Puddle's sides with his heels. She trotted through the gates, into a courtyard overlooked by the palace.

The courtyard had once been a practice ground for King Hugo's soldiers – a bright and busy home to tournaments, feasts and bustling markets. Now, all the colour and laughter was gone. Three wide tables dominated the space. A long queue of worn and haggard Avantians carrying a variety of wares, from fabrics to vegetables, from glass trinkets to trays of butchered meat, stood before each one.

There seemed to be as many soldiers in the square as citizens. Behind each table sat a man in armour clutching an iron box. More soldiers, holding pikes and swords, lurked either side of each table, and around the palace walls. Tom glanced about, but couldn't see any sign of his aunt or Captain Harkman. The villagers shuffled forwards, exchanging their bundles for coins when they reached the front of the queue. Their wares were whisked away towards the palace by more armed men, and the citizens went on their way, downcast and silent, clutching their coins.

Tom seethed with fury.

Jezrin will pay for what he has done to Avantia, he vowed.

Tom slid from Puddle's back and led her to a nearby water trough. Then he untied Aduro's baskets, and joined the end a queue behind a man stooped beneath a sack of grain.

Suddenly, a wail of despair went up from the front of his queue. "But how will I feed my family? Surely my eggs are worth twice that!" Tom looked to see a young woman with tumbling auburn curls standing before the table, her eyes bright with tears. She held her palm out before the soldier with the iron box, showing three small coins. The soldier, a fair-haired man with fierce, blue eyes glaring from his sunburned face, reached out and snatched the money back.

"If you're not happy with what you're given, you'll get nothing."

The woman gasped and dropped to her knees. "But my children! They'll starve. Please, sir, I'm sorry, three is plenty. I'll make it last. Just don't send me home empty-handed. I couldn't bear it!"

"Stop your whimpering and get out of the way." The soldier took an egg from the basket beside him, and slammed it down on her head. The egg burst, leaving a sticky spattering, speckled with shell, dripping from the woman's hair. She backed away from the table, but her foot skidded

on a rotten pear and she tumbled. A
terrible silence filled the courtyard.
The soldier picked up another egg and
took aim. Tom leapt forward, his face
burning with rage. He stood before the
table, blocking the soldier's throw.

"Move, boy," the man said, "or you'll
get more than egg on your face!"

"You have no right to treat people that way,"Tom said. He turned to the woman behind him and helped her to her feet. She bobbed him a quick curtsey, then burst into tears, scurrying away from the table with egg yolk still dripping from her hair. Tom turned back to the soldier. The man's sunburned face was redder than ever and his eyes blazed.

"You need teaching some manners!" the soldier barked, drawing his sword. He stepped out from behind the table. Tom dug his hand deep into his apple basket and clasped the hilt of his own sword, pulling it free.

Gasps went up from the citizens behind him as they backed away. The three soldiers that manned the table drew together, their blades trained on Tom.

The fair-haired soldier's lips spread into a leer. "Bringing weapons into the palace grounds is punishable by death, boy," he said. "Your days as a rebel are over." He jabbed his blade forwards.

Tom leapt aside and swung his sword hard, straight for the soldier's unarmoured throat. The man twirled his blade, catching Tom's blow and sending his sword flying. Tom spun and tried to run, but his bare feet slipped from under him on the slimy cobbles, and he sprawled forwards.

Booted feet surrounded him in an instant. A heavy knee drove into the small of his back, and rough hands gripped his arms, dragging them behind him, jerking him painfully to his feet. Tom was turned and shoved towards the table, then forced over the edge of it, a soldier holding tight to each arm. A big hand came down between his shoulder blades, pushing his chest and cheek onto the wood.

"Your head's going to join the rest up on the wall," the blue-eyed soldier growled. He stepped so close, Tom could smell the oniony stink of him. His belt buckle was right before Tom's face. Squinting up, Tom could see the soldier's head and shoulders outlined against the sky. He squirmed and kicked his legs out behind him, but was shoved harder against the wood. The only sounds in the square were the rasp of breath from the soldier

at Tom's side, and the keening cries of carrion birds awaiting their next meal. The soldier lifted his longsword with a swish.

Tom gritted his teeth, fear burning inside him. *I can't die like this! Not before I put history right!*

THE DEVOURER OF SOULS

Tom heard the scrape of a footstep from above him. Something – a pot, Tom realised – tumbled from the sky. It hurtled straight towards the soldier who stood over Tom, his sword raised high, ready for the fatal stroke.

Crack! The pot shattered on the soldier's head. The man's eyes rolled back then flickered closed. His body toppled backwards like a felled tree, and his sword clanged on the cobbles.

Tom felt the grip of the soldiers holding him slacken, just a little. It was all the chance he needed. He twisted and squirmed free of their hands, his body made strong by the adrenaline surging through him. He glanced up to see a girl wearing the brown dress and white apron of a maid, racing along a parapet. She ducked through a door into a tower, and slammed it behind her.

"Get her!" one of the guards cried. The other grabbed for Tom, but Tom vaulted onto the table and raced on, leaping from table to table, then down into the courtyard and away.

"Stop him!" a gruff voice shouted.

Tom heard a screech as a table was
shoved aside, along with nervous
laughter from the crowd. The laugher
was soon cut short by the sound of
booted feet, running – a lot of feet.
He glanced over his shoulder to see
at least five soldiers racing after him

over the cobbles. He sped onwards
towards the palace.

*They'll never catch me wearing all
that armour! And they have no idea
how well I know this place!*

Tom ducked between the stables
and the palace wall then raced
onwards, leaping over a pile of
stinking straw and swerving around
a water trough. He darted from
the shadow of a tower, into bright
sunlight, and back into shadow again,
under a walkway, then around the
side of the kitchen block. Shouts
and the *clank* of armour told him
the guards were still tailing him. He
pulled up suddenly at the sound of
more guards ahead, coming the other
way. He threw himself into an alcove,

his back to a wooden door.

"He went this way!" The shouts were getting louder.

"We'll see his head on a spike yet!"

No, you won't! Tom vowed. But with the sounds of pursuit loud on either side, he wasn't sure how he'd escape.

Suddenly, the door behind him flew open and he lurched backwards into a dimly lit room full of brooms and mops. The maid in brown and white flashed him a grin as she bolted the door. Tom gasped in wonder.

"Elenna! I've never been so pleased to see anyone in my life!"

"Me neither!" Elenna said. "What is going on? I woke in the servants' quarters this morning, and I've been piecing things together all day.

Everything's wrong, Tom. Jezrin is on the throne. Jezrin!"

Tom nodded. "I woke up in Errinel – and look at me! I've got the muscle tone of a puppy, and I can hardly hold a sword. And it's all down to Jezrin. I think he's used Tempra to change time. He went back to Hugo's coronation and had him killed. Only we remember the real past because only we drank Tempra's blood." Tom smiled suddenly – he was so relieved to see his friend after everything that had happened. "Nice dress, by the way," he said. "I never thought I'd see you working as a maid."

Elenna screwed up her face in a jokey scowl and snatched the white cap from her head, revealing her short, spiky hair. She balled up the cap and tossed it away.

"I think I've lost my job anyway," she said. Then her smile faded. "You know, all the servants live in terror of Tempra. They call it Jezrin's Beast."

Her words brought Tom back to

the horror of why he'd come to the palace. "Where are prisoners taken?" he asked Elenna.

She shuddered. "To the dungeon," she said. "And after that, they're never seen again."

"Well, that's where we're headed," Tom said. "We need to rescue Maria."

Elenna nodded. "I had a feeling you were going to say something like that. But if your aunt's down there with the Beast, we'd better hurry before it's too late."

Tom put his ear to the wooden door and listened. He could hear the soldiers talking in gruff voices.

"... not here, anyway. You go that way, and I'll interrogate the crowd."

Tom waited until their clanking

footsteps faded, then crossed to a
door on the other side of the room,
opened it, and looked out. "The coast
is clear," he told Elenna. They stole
through the doorway into the palace
complex, and scurried down a narrow
passageway. It opened into a small
inner courtyard with a pump. Tom
knew the space would be busy on
washing day, but now, it was deserted.
He glanced all around them, but even
the windows above were blank. Tom
led Elenna to a drainage grate set
into the cobbles in the corner of the
courtyard.

"You keep watch," he said. Then he
knelt and gripped the slimy metal
of the grate with his fingers. It was
heavy and awkward, but before long

he managed to push it to one side. He peered into the darkness below. A cold, dank breath of air wafted out, reeking of rats and sewage. Tom posted his legs through the hole and dropped down inside. He landed ankle-deep in cold, slimy water, wishing again he still had his boots.

Elenna landed lightly beside him. "Which way?" she asked. Damp, grimy brickwork led in either direction, lit only by the daylight from above.

"If I've got my bearings right, the dungeons should be that way," Tom said, pointing right. The passage led sharply downwards. Elenna nodded. They crept along the winding passageways and branching tunnels below the palace.

Eventually, the passageway widened to a corridor, lined with doorways barred with iron. Torches flickered in sconces on the walls. Tom and Elenna peered through the bars of the first door. Tom leapt back in

shock. Elenna gasped. Pressed into the dark shadows at the back of the cell, at least twenty people stood in silence, huddled together, their eyes glinting in the candlelight.

"I'll get you out!" Tom said, drawing the bolt on the door. The door swung open, but instead of crowding forwards, the people just stared ahead.

"What's wrong with them?" Tom said, turning to Elenna. But before she could answer, anguished cries of terror tore through the air, coming from down the passageway, making Tom's heart clench.

"Aunt Maria!" he said, gasping.

Tom raced towards Maria's screams, pounding over damp stone with Elenna at his heels. He turned a sharp corner in the tunnel just as the last echo of his aunt's screams died away. Tom froze. A huge, writhing shadow on the wall flexed and bulged, flickering in the torchlight. A pair of guards stood before the hideous shape, holding the limp body of Tom's aunt. Tom started forwards, but Elenna grabbed his arm and pulled him into a dark doorway. A moment later, the guards bundled past, carrying Maria. Her eyes stared vacantly ahead, open yet unseeing. The sight was like a punch to Tom's guts. He doubled in pain, sickness rising in his throat, and a black curtain of hopelessness crashing down around him.

I'm too late, he realised. *Tempra has stolen her soul.*

CAPTIVES

"While there is blood in my veins," Tom said, his voice husky with emotion, "Jezrin will pay for this." He strained to charge after the soldiers, but Elenna kept his arm in a firm grip.

"Wait!" she said. "We need a plan!"

Tom shook her hand away. The anger and pain inside him wouldn't let him wait. He broke into a run. Elenna's footsteps soon joined his own. Tom led her back the way they had come, past the cells of mindless people. He daren't look. He couldn't let himself see his aunt in among the others. Finally, he reached the patch of pale sunlight shining through the hole from the courtyard above. He put his hands on the edge of the hole and heaved himself through. The courtyard was deserted. Tom thrust a hand down and hauled Elenna up into daylight.

"That way," he said, pointing to a door on the far side of the courtyard. "We'll take the servants' stairs to the throne room."

Elenna shook her head. "You can't just burst in," she said. "It's guarded."

"I have to try!" Tom said. He raced

across the courtyard and shoved the door, tumbling into a dim passageway. It led to the servants' stairs, which Tom took two at a time. His breath rasped in his throat, and he could hear Elenna panting behind him, but he forced himself to keep running.

The stairs opened onto a wider corridor lined with tapestries. Tom and Elenna followed it past more narrow flights of stairs leading from the kitchens and guard room. Tom stopped at a corner and peered around it, towards a pair of gilded doors – entrance to the throne room. Soldiers stood either side of the doors, plumed helms on their heads and long pikes in their hands.

Tom ducked his head back round

the corner to see Elenna watching
him with an exasperated frown, her
cheeks pink from running. "See?" she
said. "You can't just walk in there.
You'll be cut to pieces." Tom felt the
desperate gulf of hopelessness opening
inside him again. To be so close … He
had to get in. He had to get revenge!
Something in his expression made
Elenna's frown soften.

"All right," she said. "I'll get you
inside. Wait here." A table stood part
way along the corridor to the throne
room, bearing a tray with a crystal jug.
Elenna strode around the corner and
picked it up, then carried it towards
the gilded doors. When she reached
them she turned to the guards.

"Water for His Majesty!" she

said, bobbing a curtsy. The two men
frowned and crossed their pikes over
the doors.

"No one called for water," one said,
his voice rumbling with menace.
Elenna didn't falter. She ducked her
head beneath their crossed pikes and
pushed at a door. It swung open.

"Hey!" the first guard cried, while
the other grabbed Elenna's shoulder
and yanked her back. Elenna
stumbled, and the tray in her hands
flew up into the air, dowsing both men
with water. The jug and tray landed
with a crash. Elenna sprinted away.

"Stop, wench! Clean up this mess!"
one of the guards cried. The other
started after her down the corridor.
Both had their backs to Tom.

Nicely done, Elenna!

Tom streaked along the passageway, through the open throne room door, and slammed it shut behind him, barring it with an echoing clunk. The room was empty. Hugo's throne stood as Tom remembered it, on a raised dais towards the rear wall, bathed in light from the stained glass windows behind it. But where the room used to be decorated with paintings of all the kings of old, now just one picture dominated the space. It showed a young Hugo on his knees with his sword raised as if to defend himself. He looked frightened as Jezrin towered over him, his black eyes glinting with victory.

Tom turned away from the vile image, towards an archway to his right, covered with a thick red curtain. From inside, he could hear an animal-like chomping, slurping sound. He peered through the curtain and saw an enormously fat man seated at the end of a dining table, his back to the door. The man wore a crown on his thinning curls, and a billowing purple robe. Pillowy rolls of fat bulged over the side of his chair. *Jezrin*. He was old and fat, but Tom would recognise his enemy anywhere. The wizard's face was bent low over his plate, his teeth ripping noisily at a leg of mutton.

Tom crossed the room in quick, silent strides and snatched up the sharp knife from the table, sliding it under the wizard's grey beard.

Jezrin stopped eating and drew a sharp breath.

"Put your hands on the table," Tom said. "Don't move. Don't make a sound, and don't even think of using magic."

"Young Tom?" Jezrin said, easing his greasy hands slowly onto the table before him. "You have caught me quite by surprise." The wizard's sneering voice was reedy and nasal.

"I drank Tempra's blood before the changes you made took effect," Tom said. "I know what you did, and I remember everything. It's time to put an end to this charade."

"I quite agree," Jezrin said, his jowls waggling as he spoke. "But I think you've forgotten something."

"What's that?" Tom asked.

"My apprentice," Jezrin said.

Tom was blinded by a flash of white light. Jezrin's elbow landed in his gut, throwing him back. A terrible burning pain seared through Tom's body, making his limbs jerk. The knife dropped from his shaking hand. His legs folded beneath him and he tumbled to the ground. When the pain finally receded, Tom tried to stand, but found that bands of silver light bound his arms tightly to his body. He bucked and strained against the magical bonds, but they didn't budge.

I can't move my arms!

In the corner of the room, a curtain over an alcove twitched aside. A horribly familiar figure stepped out – tall and slender, wearing a long green robe and a cruel grin. *Malvel.*

Jezrin turned his bloated face towards Malvel and smiled. "This is the boy I told you about," Jezrin said. "My old enemy, Tom."

Malvel stepped forwards, a scornful
smirk playing across his sharp
features. "Him?" he asked, nudging
Tom's body with the tip of his boot.
"He's nothing but a whelp."

Tom heaved against his chains,

straining his back and chest, but it was no use. He was soon bundled over a guard's shoulder, and carried back to the dungeons. Malvel led the way, a flaming torch in his hand. They reached an empty cell, and the guard dropped Tom onto the cold, hard cobbles. Without his arms to break his fall, Tom's shoulder smashed into the ground, knocking the air from his chest. He rolled over, wheezing, to find Malvel glaring down at him.

"I've heard so much about you," Malvel said. "I expected a formidable foe, but instead I find myself confronted by a skinny, snivelling child." He glanced at the guards. "Shackle this brat."

The silver bands of light binding

Tom's arms to his body suddenly vanished. But before he could flex his aching shoulders, or even take a breath, his wrists were shoved roughly into a pair of iron manacles chained to the wall. The manacles clinked shut. Malvel shot Tom a spiteful parting smile, before gliding from the room, taking his torch with him. The two armoured guards followed, slamming the cell door, and barring it with a *clank*.

Tom stared into the gloom left in their wake, the afterimage of the torches still dancing in his vision. Then he heard a sound that made his flesh creep. It was coming from an archway to his right: a low, shuffling sound like the slither of a snake – or

lots of snakes. A moment later, a vast,
dark shape blocked the archway. It
slithered forwards and Tom shuddered.
A tangle of tapering, snaking limbs,
covered in suckers, protruded from a
round body that was dominated by a
single, bulging eye. It stared at Tom,

a sickly bluish, jelly-like mass with a single pupil filled with spite and rage. *Tempra!*

Tom shrank back against the slimy wall. *It's over,* he realised. *Avantia was relying on me, and I have failed.*

STORY TWO

Greetings, subjects.

My flag flies from the palace towers, and all of Avantia rests within my iron grip. With Tempra's help, time is at my command. My enemies are in disarray.

Tom should have stayed in his village and foraged in the dirt like the other peasants. Better to live a life as a worthless ant, than die a tiger.

What am I saying? I am GLAD the fool took me on. At this very moment he is chained before Tempra. By the time I've finished feasting, my Beast will have feasted too – devouring Tom's soul. Perhaps I will have the boy's mindless body brought to my throne room, so he can watch me rule the kingdom he loves so dearly.

Kneel before me!

Jezrin

1

RACING FROM EVIL

Tempra's bloodshot eye stared
hungrily at Tom as the Beast slithered
across the cell, one snaking tentacle
raised, groping towards his face. Tom
tugged hard against his iron cuffs,
but it was no use. He lifted his bound
hands to shield his face. Tempra slunk
closer. The Beast's vast, round eye
bulged outwards, pulsing with the
flow of blood through her veins. A vile

stink like the cold mud at the bottom of an open grave came from her in waves. The slither of muscular limbs on the stone floor sent shivers down Tom's spine. A long tentacle, tipped with a livid sucker, probed towards him, ready to feast on his soul. Tom thought of all the people he had let down. His uncle and aunt … Captain Harkman … King Hugo … all of the vile Beast's victims.

Suddenly, Tom heard a grunt, then a clang as the cell door burst open, showing the slim silhouette of a girl. An arrow whizzed past Tempra's bloodshot eye, then hit the wall and clattered to the ground. Tempra let out a hiss, her tentacles recoiling as her vast bulk shrank back into the shadows.

Elenna stepped into the room, a bow

in one hand and a bunch of keys in
the other. "Missed," she huffed.

Tom grinned, giddy with relief.
"Close enough," he said. "You saved
me from a fate worse than death!"

Elenna smiled and ran a hand
through her short, dark hair. "I'm
starting to feel more like my old self,

but my aim isn't what it used to be.
I found a bow in the weapons store."
She knelt before Tom and unlocked
the shackles about his wrists. "Now,
let's get out of here before the guards
work out what's going on."

Tom staggered to his feet and shook
his arms to get the blood flowing,
while thinking of a route to safety.

The sound of booted feet thudded
towards them, and a gruff voice cried
out: "She went that way!"

Tom and Elenna raced from the
cell, down the corridor, away from the
voices. Tom's bare feet hardly made
a sound on the stone, and Elenna
moved as quietly and swiftly as ever
in her maid's slippers.

Tom led Elenna through winding

passages, further beneath the palace. "I know a way out of here," he told her, "through the Gallery of Tombs." They raced past more barred doors, crowded with silent people. Tom didn't slow. He knew of no way to help those unlucky souls. Finally, they reached the blind end of a long, low-ceilinged corridor. Tom scanned the cracked brickwork, worried for a moment that his escape route wouldn't be there. Then he spotted a familiar grey stone, protruding slightly further than the others. He pushed it, and the wall swung open revealing a dimly lit chamber beyond.

"I never knew there was a secret way in," said Elenna.

"Nor did I until recently," said Tom.

"Aduro showed me. The old Aduro, that is."

Tom stepped through with Elenna close behind him. What he saw in the ancient tomb stirred anger inside him so powerful it stopped him in his tracks. The vaulted chamber had once been a resting place for kings, masters and Beasts alike. Now the mosaic floor lay buried under a tumble of broken stone. The tombs on either side were cracked, their fine carvings destroyed. Many had been opened.

"How dare Jezrin dishonour Avantia's heroes like this?" Tom growled.

Elenna stared at the devastation, her eyes solemn in the flickering candlelight.

"Jezrin and Malvel will stop at nothing to get what they want," she said. "We should leave the palace, and find somewhere safe to think."

Tom thought of Jezrin, stuffing food into his bloated face, while in the darkness below him, innocent citizens lost everything they were to his vile Beast. *How can I just leave, knowing more people will suffer?*

But in his heart, Tom knew Elenna was right. He nodded.

They headed up a long, winding stairway that led from the desecrated tombs to the stable block above. The stuffy warmth and scent of hay was welcome after the unearthly chill underground. Horses scuffed at wooden boards as Tom and Elenna passed, and Tom wondered what had become of Puddle. *I'll come back for her later, when all this is over,* he vowed to himself.

They reached the final partition, and the horse inside suddenly snorted. Its great hooves crashed down on the wood and it let out a desperate whinny. Tom recognised the sound. *But it can't be!* He lifted the bar to the door and threw it open. The black stallion inside pressed forwards to greet him, nuzzling its nose into the palms of Tom's outstretched hands. The blaze of white on the horse's forehead, shaped like an arrow, confirmed Tom's hopes. *Storm!* His beloved steed. Even across a chasm of broken time, their bond remained.

"They're coming!" Elenna cried.
Sure enough, Tom could hear the
shouts of running armoured men in
the courtyard outside.

He vaulted onto Storm's bare
back. Storm shied at the unfamiliar
sensation, but Tom placed a calming
hand on his flank, and the stallion

settled. Elenna hurried to Storm's side, and Tom gave her his hand, helping her up behind him. Once they were seated, Tom touched his heels to Storm's sides. Storm leapt forward and Tom felt a rush of joy at the instant surge of speed. Elenna gripped Tom's waist as they burst through the stable door into the courtyard. Villagers and soldiers turned to stare as Storm pounded over the cobbles towards the gates.

"Men! Aim and fire!" Captain Harkman's stern voice called from the battlements above. Tom leaned over Storm's back and dug in his heels. Storm's stride lengthened and the wind whooshed past as the mighty stallion sped onwards.

Arrows clattered against the cobbles all around them as Storm ducked beneath the portcullis. A pair of guards tried to bar their way with long pikes, but Storm didn't falter and they quickly dived aside with cries of fear. The thunder of Storm's hooves echoed across the drawbridge as he carried Tom and Elenna out of the City. Tom felt Elenna's grip on his waist shift as she turned to look behind them.

"We've got company!" she cried, her voice snatched at by the wind.

Tom glanced over his shoulder and cursed under his breath. A host of mounted soldiers were pouring through gates after them, surrounded by clouds of rising dust.

2

A STEED AND A SWORD

Tom leaned into the wind, feeling the rhythm of Storm's hooves pounding through his body. Elenna clung tightly to his waist. Tom could hear the clatter of the soldiers' horses behind them. But without a saddle or armour to weigh him down, Storm was swifter than any horse, even with two passengers. *We can outrun them!* Tom thought.

But then a stooped, hooded figure stepped into the road before him, one hand raised.

"Move!" Tom bellowed.

The figure didn't budge. He raised both hands and a glowing green ball of energy sparked into life between

his palms. Then the figure flicked the magical orb towards Tom, Elenna and Storm. It sped through the air in a glittering arc, and exploded in a starburst of green sparks over them. Storm slowed to a stop as the sparks formed a transparent green dome. Tom peered through it and saw the soldiers following them drawing up.

"Where did they go?" he heard one cry. "They were right here!"

"He's made us invisible!" Elenna breathed in wonder.

Tom looked back to the figure, seeing him throw back his hood.

Aduro! The hermit-wizard was looking up at Tom, his old face glowing with pleasure.

"I wasn't sure that would work!"

he said brightly. "It won't last forever, though. We'd better get going, but not before you introduce me to your young friend."

Tom turned to find Elenna grinning. "This is Elenna," he said. "She's your friend as well as mine."

Aduro dipped his head to Elenna. "A pleasure to meet you," he said.

Tom could hear angry shouting from the soldiers on the path. "But we can't go back!" One man's frightened voice rose above the rest. "Jezrin will feed us to his Beast."

Another soldier sounded angry, as he said: "They must have got help from the rebels. We'll hunt them down."

That seemed to settle the argument. The soldiers clattered on down the road, soon disappearing into the low glare of the setting sun.

Aduro beckoned to Tom and Elenna. "Come with me," he said.

A chill wind moaned through the crooked branches of Aduro's apple trees as the last glint of golden sunlight trickled from the sky. The shadows beneath the trees had deepened from violet to black, and the birds had long since quietened their song for the night. Elenna tugged her cloak closer, raised her bow about her and then let an arrow fly. It sliced through the heart of an apple.

"Perfect shot!" Tom said.

He saw the flash of Elenna's teeth in the gloom as she turned with a grin. "I think I'll call it a day," she said. "I can hardly see!" They had made no fire, just in case its light gave their location away.

Aduro sat watching them, seated on a fallen trunk, his chin resting on his fist.

"There must be a way of beating Jezrin!" Tom said. "We've done it before, in our own time."

Aduro sighed. "In this reality, we've had no such success. We've been fighting Jezrin for years and we're getting nowhere."

"We?" said Elenna.

"I wasn't sure what I could tell Tom before," Aduro replied, his eyes twinkling. "But not everyone in Avantia is content to let Jezrin rule over them."

"The rebels?" Tom asked, remembering what the soldier had said.

Aduro nodded. "There are too few of us. People are afraid to stand up against Jezrin and his soldiers. And

with Malvel too, not to mention the
Beast that lies beneath the palace …
We just don't stand a chance."

Frustration welled in Tom's chest.
This was not the Aduro he knew. "It's
got nothing to do with numbers!" Tom
said. "It's about courage. Elenna and
I have fought many battles and won,
just the two of us. In the world I came
from, you were more than a match for
Malvel."

Aduro shook his head sadly
and spread his hands. "This is not
your world, Tom. Malvel was my
apprentice until Jezrin lured him
away with promises of power. Now
his magic is strong, but he practises
nothing but evil."

"Well, if we can't outnumber Jezrin

and his men," Elenna said, "we'll have to outsmart them. Something tells me the answer to this puzzle lies with Tempra. All this started when the sands of time started to run backwards."

Tom nodded, his eyes on the knotty branches of an apple tree, black against the starry sky. "But now King Hugo is dead, nothing can ever be as it was," he said. "Unless ..." He sprang to his feet and crossed to the tree, an idea forming. "Unless we can cut off this sick and distorted branch of time." He traced his finger along a twisted branch, back to where it split into two forks. "If we get rid of this fork, time will flow back along its original path."

Aduro was on his feet now too, his eyes bright in the darkness. "Of course!" he said. "Jezrin must have used Tempra to go back in time. The ancient texts said that Tempra is always hungry for souls. Maybe Jezrin promised her a feast in return for doing his will."

"A feast on the souls of innocent people!" Tom said, balling his fists as he thought of his aunt's lifeless eyes after Tempra had finished with her. "But it's going to end now. I'm going to vanquish the Beast, and force her to put time back as it should be. Then none of this evil will have happened."

"It's a good plan," Elenna said, "but the palace is guarded like a fortress. We'll never get inside again without being seen by the soldiers."

Tom grinned and caught Aduro's eye. "We will if we're invisible," he said.

Aduro arched an eyebrow and smiled. "I knew there was something about you, young man!" he said. "Come with me, I want to give you a gift."

Aduro led Tom between shadowy boughs until they reached an ancient tree, leafless and sprouting with fungus. Aduro pointed to a gaping hole in the trunk.

"Reach inside," he said.

Tom stepped towards the tree. A twig snapped beneath his foot, sending a bird squawking from its roost. The rich smell of loam and rotting wood wafted from the hole.

Tom reached his hand inside, half expecting to feel the tickle of insects or the soft touch of fur. Instead, his fingers fell on cold, hard steel – the hilt of a sword. And not just any sword! Tom drew out the weapon, feeling the familiar weight of it in his hand. He swished it through the air.

"My sword!" Tom said. "But how?"

"I took it when I fled the palace, hoping that one day I would find a new Master of the Beasts to wield it. That day is today."

Tom felt a weight of responsibility settle on his shoulders. It felt good – like a well-worn cloak. *This is what I was born for!* Tom thought. He turned to Aduro, and bowed his head.

"While there is blood in my veins, I will not let you down!"

3

TRAITOR TO THE CROWN

Tom, Elenna and Storm rode hard towards the palace, the moonlit landscape around them tinted green by Aduro's shield of invisibility. Before long, the City's walls came into view. The skulls that decorated the ramparts shone cold and pale beneath the stars. Although it was night, the gates stood open. Blazing torchlight flooded out.

"Something's going on," Elenna said. "I wonder what?"

A steady stream of villagers ducked through the gates, their features hidden by cloaks.

"Nothing good, we can be sure of that," Tom said. He slowed Storm to a trot as they passed close to a group of citizens.

"Is it true he's been captured?" Tom heard a hushed voice ask.

"They say they found his hiding place," a woman said, her voice choked with anger and dread. "If they did, all hope is lost."

Tom, Storm and Elenna approached the gates unseen, protected by their magical shield. When they reached the marketplace, they found that a wooden stage had been erected against the palace walls. The citizens pressed close around it.

Captain Harkman stood at the centre of the stage, flanked by armed soldiers. At his feet knelt a tall man in travel-worn leathers. A sack covered his face, but his head was held high.

Captain Harkman lifted his hand, and a soldier at his side banged his sword on his shield.

"Silence!" the soldier cried. Once the murmur of voices had quietened, Harkman began to speak.

"For decades, the leader of the rebel militia has evaded our capture," he said. "He has tormented King Jezrin's forces and committed crimes too numerous to list." Harkman clenched

his fist. "But now, he kneels before you all, a broken man. Today will be a lesson to all traitors to the crown. There is no escape. You will be caught and we will show you no mercy!"

A roar of cheers went up from the soldiers on the platform.

"Tempra! Come forth!" Captain

Harkman cried. Tom felt a tingle across the back of his neck as a shadow slithered from an alcove behind the stage. Terrified gasps whispered through the crowd as the vile form of Tempra emerged into the torchlight. The hideous Beast glided on her long muscular limbs, her flesh rasping over the stage and her bulging eye fixed on the hooded man.

A sick dread rose in Tom's stomach. He glanced at the soldiers flanking Harkman, wondering if he could reach the prisoner in time.

Harkman's hand fell to the hood of the man at his side, and he glanced up at a balcony overlooking the stage. Tom followed his gaze, to see two cloaked forms, one bloated and one slim, step out onto the moonlit platform. *Jezrin and Malvel!* Jezrin leaned forwards, his hands tight on the balcony rail and a hungry light in his eyes. He gave a nod. Harkman snatched the hood from the kneeling man, revealing a weather-beaten, bearded face, with straight

eyebrows and eyes that blazed defiance.

Tom felt dizzy. The courtyard swam before his eyes. He couldn't breathe. Beside him Elenna whispered a single word, filled with shocked dismay.

"Taladon!"

4

A MIGHTY BATTLE RAGES

I knew my father was no coward, Tom thought. *He's the leader of the rebels!*

But his relief was quickly swamped by an icy rage as he was drawn back to another time and place – a time when he'd watched Taladon die, struck down by the White Knight of Forton. Tom had felt the same way then. Too far away and too weak to help his father. But then he gritted his teeth and pulled himself tall, drawing on all his strength of will. *I won't let this happen! Not again.*

Tempra reached out with a tentacle towards Taladon's head.

"I'm stopping this now!" Tom told Elenna, his eyes fixed on the brave face of his father.

Elenna lifted her bow and strung an arrow. "I'll cover you," she said.

Tom pushed into the crowd of citizens, still enclosed in his green shield of invisibility. The stage was soon lost to view in a sea of closely packed bodies. Tom shoved between threadbare cloaks, elbowing sinewy men and haggard women aside, ignoring their shouts of surprise and anger, not stopping until he reached the front.

Already, one of Tempra's suckers was attached to Taladon's forehead. *No!* Tom vaulted onto the stage. His father's face was contorted, his eyes screwed shut and his teeth clenched.

An arrow streaked over the stage and slammed into Tempra's tentacle with a thunk. Tempra drew back her wounded limb, leaving a trail of blood on the wood and a purple mark on Taladon's skin.

"What's going on?" Harkman snapped. Tom raced across the stage, pulling his sword from his belt as Tempra fastened a new sucker to Taladon's head.

Snick! Tom brought his blade down

hard on Tempra's slimy limb.

The Beast let out a high, keening screech, shrinking towards the back of the stage in a flowing tumble of limbs. Taladon crumpled forwards into a ball. At the same moment, the green glow that coloured Tom's vision disappeared. Aduro's shield was gone! Tom raced to his father's side, not caring who could see him. He cradled Taladon's head in his lap. "Father! Are you all right?"

Taladon's face was deathly pale and beaded with sweat. His eyes were closed. *Please don't let it be too late!*

"Seize the boy!" Tom heard Harkman cry, but then another arrow whistled through the air and the captain leapt from the stage, just before it ploughed into the wood right where he'd been standing.

"I'm coming, Tom!" Elenna cried.
Tom caught a glimpse of her pressing
towards the stage, before she
disappeared into the crowd.

Heavy footsteps pounded over
the stage, and Tom turned to see
Harkman's soldiers storming towards
him, swords drawn. Tom thrust his
own sword out awkwardly over his
father's body.

"Don't come any closer!" he cried.

At the same moment, a great
shout went up from the market
square below. "For Taladon!" Tom
looked down to see men and women
throwing back their cloaks, revealing
glinting weapons. The rest of the
citizens scattered as the rebels

pressed towards the stage.

"Kill the rebels!" Captain Harkman cried, lunging towards a thickset, bearded man with an axe. The soldiers on the stage spun and leapt down to meet their attackers – all but one, who sprang towards Tom and Taladon.

Suddenly, a slender, dark-haired woman vaulted onto the stage, her eyes flashing with fury.

"Leave them!" she cried, swinging her sword at the soldier's back. It hit the man's armour with a clunk, sending him tumbling from the wooden platform. The woman hurried after him.

Tom scanned the chaos, looking for a safe place to take his father. He caught sight of Elenna wielding her bow like a staff as a soldier lunged towards her, but then she was lost again in the heaving mass of bodies and glinting weapons.

All around, the flair of fires sprung up across the square. Tom glanced behind him, hoping to see a door to the palace left unguarded. What he saw instead chilled him to the bone.

Jezrin stood still and silent in the shadows at the back of the stage. As the wizard's eyes locked with Tom's, he smiled and lifted his staff. Purple energy burst from the tip. Before Tom could move, the energy slammed into the stage before him with a crack. His arms were ripped from his father's body as the blast threw them both up into the air. Tom tumbled, his limbs

flailing, fragments of wood and smoke
swirling around him as he tried to
right himself.

BOOF! Hard stone slammed into his
back, punching the breath from his
lungs. He tried to scramble up, but
his leg buckled, and a sharp pain in his
thigh left him gasping for breath. He
glanced down to see a thick splinter, as

long as his finger, poking from
his flesh. Gritting his teeth, he
pulled it free and threw it aside,
then clambered to his feet. He couldn't
see Jezrin. All around Tom, the battle
raged. The *clunk* and *crash* of metal
on metal filled the air. Tom looked
frantically for his father and saw his
crumpled body nearby in the shadow
of the palace wall. In three long strides
he was at his father's side. *You can't
be dead!*

Tom was relieved to see Taladon's
chest moving. He tucked his arms
under his father's shoulders and
heaved, pulling him up to lean against
the rampart wall.

The sounds of fighting continued,
grunts and cries of anger and pain.

But for Tom, the sounds seemed far away, while the rasp of his father's breath and the sight of his pale, strong features were everything.

Taladon's eyes flickered open. As they focused on Tom's face, the expression of pain and confusion left them, and they softened to a smile.

"My son ..." he said. His voice was little more than a croak but it was full of wonder, of love. Tears filled Tom's eyes. He had never thought he would see his father again.

"What a touching scene!" a harsh voice sneered. Tom turned to see a tall, cloaked figure standing only paces away, his hands raised, red energy crackling in his palms. *Malvel.* "How fitting that you will die together!" the

Dark Wizard said. "My fire is powerful enough to melt steel like butter. Prepare yourselves for agony."

"Not so fast!" Aduro suddenly appeared in a flash of green light, two balls of bright energy glowing in his hands. He strode towards Malvel, his eyes ablaze with anger.

"My old master!" Malvel said, his smile broadening. "It seems today I will finish all my enemies at once!"

The Dark Wizard hurled the sizzling energy bolts in his hands towards Aduro, who responded with his own magic. Two deadly beams, one red and one green, met in the air between the wizards with a crash that echoed off the palace walls. A blinding flash illuminated the battle all around.

Tom saw Aduro grit his teeth, his face creased with effort. Malvel's smile became a grimace. The bright beams of red and green energy sizzled and sparked between the wizards' outstretched hands. Malvel took a step forwards, then another, forcing Aduro back. Tom could see the light of victory in the Dark Wizard's eyes.

Aduro strained against the red energy, his elbows bent and his back bowed as he dug his heels into the ground. He closed his eyes, and suddenly forced himself upright, pushing his arms outwards. A roar burst from his lips, and a flash of green light filled the courtyard as Malvel was flung backwards through the air, crashing through the base of a tower. The tower toppled forwards, crumbling in a cascade of stone and dust, burying the wizard.

Aduro sank to his knees. Tom glanced at his father, to see his dark eyes clear and focused.

"Go to Aduro," Taladon said.

Tom raced towards the wizard, but he lifted a hand and shook his head. "I will be fine," he said. "You must fight Tempra." Aduro pointed towards the palace, beyond the broken stage. In the shadow of the stable block, Tom could see the sinewy limbs of the Beast coiled in the darkness.

Tom lifted his sword and skirted the palace wall, past the broken tower where Malvel lay buried, the furious battle still raging all around him.

Crack! Something lashed across his shins, sending him sprawling. Tom scrambled up to see Jezrin step from beneath an arch, his eyes glinting cruelly in the firelight.

He pointed the tip of his staff at Tom. "I won't let a peasant boy steal my kingdom," he said, his words hissing between clenched teeth. "I won it fair and square when I killed Hugo."

Tom sprang, his sword lifted to

strike. "There's nothing fair about treachery and murder," he shouted, slashing at the wizard's chest. His blade connected with something in the air before Jezrin's cloak, the impact sending a shockwave of pain up Tom's arm. *He's wearing invisible armour!*

Jezrin flicked the tip of his staff. A red bolt of energy seared through the air, catching Tom in an agonising embrace and lifting him above the battle-bound courtyard.

Below him, Jezrin's face shone in the light of countless fires raging across the square. Jezrin tipped back his head, letting out a long cackle of laughter. "When I let you fall," he cried, "you will break every bone in your puny body!"

5

FIGHTING WITH FIRE

Tom hung helpless in the air, watching the wizard's jowls quiver as the cruel laughter went on and on. Tom could hardly breathe for the agony of Jezrin's evil fire burning through his body. He bit his lip to stop himself crying out in pain. Below him, soldiers and rebels hacked mercilessly at each other while the palace burned. Finally, Jezrin's laughter faded. The wizard drew back his staff, ready to send Tom plummeting to his death. But then, on pounding hooves, a horse barged headfirst into the wizard.

Puddle!

The nag bowled the wizard over, then gave a frantic whinny. Jezrin's staff flew from his hand. The red energy beam that sizzled from its tip, holding Tom suspended high above the courtyard, lashed like a whip, then vanished. Tom felt a jolt, his stomach lurching as he was thrown backwards through the air.

He plunged down towards the burning stables, crackling orange flames rising up to meet him.

Tom fell through the blazing stable roof and landed in a pile of straw. He lay for a moment, winded, gasping for breath in the smoky air. All around him horses screamed in terror and beat their hooves against the wooden partitions. Through the open stable door, he could see Jezrin's bloated form grappling with Taladon. Beyond them, Elenna ducked a vicious blow from Harkman's sword, then swung a huge axe at his chest. Tom scrambled up and dived towards the doorway, his own sword held high.

But then a powerful blow slapped the blade from his hand. A strong, lithe tentacle snapped about his ankle and tugged. *Oof!* Tom landed hard on his stomach. He glanced over his shoulder to see Tempra's eye staring at him. He kicked out, trying to free his foot from the Beast, but her grip was too strong. His fingers scrabbled in the straw for his fallen sword. Before he could reach it, however, the Beast jerked him back into the flickering shadows. A thick tentacle with glistening suckers groped towards his face. Tom tried to push it away, but it flowed around his hands like cold, wet mud. He felt a clammy pressure on his forehead. *No!* Everything around him dissolved in a sickening swirl of red and black. A terrible searing pain filled his head. The sounds around him faded into a rush of wind.

A memory flashed before his eyes. A broad figure clad in gold armour lying wounded, eyes squeezed shut as red blood flowed across the ground. *Taladon. Dead.* Then another picture. An armoured woman this time, tall and slender. Tom's mother Freya. That memory too was whisked away, and

a new image filled Tom's mind – the
face of a skinny girl, peering out
from between gnarled branches. Her
short dark hair stood up in messy
tufts, and scratches covered her skin.
Panic raged inside him as he tried

to remember the girl's name. *Ella? Ellie?* Then the image vanished into darkness. He tried to find another memory to take its place, but all he could see was an inky pit of empty black nothingness. The only sensation left to him was the terrible burning inside his mind.

Tempra is taking my soul ...

Tom forced himself to focus on the hot, biting agony of it, boring into a point between his brows. He became aware of his shaking body, of a tight pressure around his ankle. He could hear the terrible scream of horses and men in pain. He forced his aching eyes to open. A purplish orb bulged and pulsed before him, red veins snaking outwards from a pupil as black as night. A tiny image gazed back at him from the pupil, reflected in its depths. A boy, with wide eyes and a thick tentacle fastened between his brows. *It's me!* Tom realised. *I'm Tom. And I am Avantia's Master of the Beasts!*

He thrashed against Tempra's tentacles with all his might. He scrabbled in the dirt with his hands, looking for a weapon. His fingers gripped something – a length of blackened wood, still smouldering at one end. Tom bent his arm and drove the smoking tip straight towards Tempra's eye.

Tempra hissed, cringing back from the wooden spike, releasing Tom. He leapt to his feet. His sword lay before

him, glimmering in the firelight.
He snatched it up, then rounded on
the Beast. Tempra cowered against
the stable wall, her snaking limbs
raised to protect her eye. Tom
swung his sword. *Thunk!* A coiled
limb tumbled to the ground, sliced

from the Beast's body.

Snick! Tom cut another writhing tentacle free. His blade danced in the firelight, cutting and slicing, until all Tempra's soul-sucking limbs were lying in the straw before him. Then he stopped, breathing heavily, and looked into the Beast's terrified eye.

"Take me back to where all of this began," Tom demanded. The Beast's monstrous lid squeezed shut, covering her bulging yellow orb.

"Agh!" A high-pitched cry sliced through the panicked screaming of horses and the crackle of fire. Tom turned. For a moment he couldn't believe what he was seeing.

Elenna lay on her back with her limbs spread and her eyes closed.

Captain Harkman towered over her. The tip of his sword was red with blood.

She's ... dead ...

Tom turned back to the Beast.

"Do it now!" he cried. Tempra's vast eye flicked open, but this time a bright blue light swirled in its depths. The light grew brighter and paler, filling the stable, bathing Tom in an icy white glare with the burning touch of freezing water. The sounds of battle faded, and Tom toppled forwards into a pale tunnel of light.

HUGO'S CORONATION

Tom opened his eyes to bright
sunlight, his nose twitching at the
smell of roasting meat. He squinted
into the light, and found he was in
the palace courtyard. Everything was
different. The fighting and the fires
were gone. Bright bunting decorated
the towers, and a banner hung above
the open palace door.

All hail, King Hugo, Tom read.

Tempra has sent me back to Hugo's coronation day! Tom glanced around the deserted courtyard, to see more bunting, and wreaths of flowers. A few paces away, a spinning white light hung in the air. *The portal!*

A hissing voice spoke in Tom's mind. *Hurry, Master of the Beasts!* Tempra said. *I cannot hold this portal open for long.* Tom dashed across the courtyard and through the open palace door. The hum of distant voices and the clink of glasses led him along a corridor to the main dining hall. He burst through the archway to find a table laden with platters of steaming food running the length of the room. Crystal goblets glittered in the light from blazing torches. All around the table, richly dressed guests ate and drank, while guards stood by in the shadows.

A guard stepped out before Tom. "Stop!" he said, gesturing at Tom's sword. "No weapons allowed in here."

Tom peered past him. At the far end of the table, King Hugo sat on a raised seat. He was younger than Tom had ever seen him. His cheeks were flushed and his eyes shone as he gazed at his guests. Aduro was at Hugo's side, his hair as shiny and black as a raven's wings. Tom couldn't see any sign of Jezrin.

"Boy." The guard's voice drew Tom's attention. "Give me the sword, and you can join the feast. But hurry, I must find the king's squire – you're so alike, for a moment I thought you were him."

Tom handed his sword to the guard and stepped further into the room. *Maybe the past is already mended,* he thought, watching the merry feasting before him as the guard hurried away.

At the end of the table, Aduro got to his feet, and chimed a knife against his glass. A hush fell.

"A toast!" Aduro said. He lifted a crystal flask, filled with amber liquid. "To our new king, on behalf of the Circle of Wizards who have kindly sent this wine – a rare vintage fermented from grapes of the mystical vines of Henkrall." Aduro pulled the cork from the bottle and tipped a golden stream into the king's goblet.

Hugo swirled the wine in his glass

and took a long sniff. He smiled.
"Mmm. It smells delightful," he said,
raising his glass towards a tall, cloaked
figure at the far end of the table, near
to where Tom stood. Something about
the posture of the figure, and his long,
curled hair sent a spike of fear along
Tom's spine.

It's Jezrin! he realised. Time seemed
to slow as Hugo lifted his glass
towards his lips.

7

FULL CIRCLE

"Don't drink it!" Tom shouted, diving forwards. He barged between two seated men and leapt onto the table, sending plates and cutlery clattering to the ground.

Shouts of alarm erupted all around as he raced along the table, scattering food and glasses. King Hugo watched, open-mouthed, the cup of golden liquid hovering before his lips.

Tom hurled himself forwards and dashed the cup from Hugo's hand. Immediately, he felt a pair of strong arms circle his waist. He was dragged from the table and spun around to face a boy who looked to be a few years older than Tom. He had light brown hair, high cheekbones and strong, straight brows, just like …

Just like me, Tom thought. *He's my father!*

"What is the meaning of this?" King Hugo boomed. Taladon held Tom's arms tight, and turned him to face the king. The room was silent, every eye fixed on Tom.

"The wine was poisoned, Your Majesty," Tom said.

"Ridiculous!" King Hugo, cried. "Why, the bottle has only just been opened, right before my eyes."

"My lord!" Aduro cut in, his voice sharp with alarm. "Look!" He pointed down at the tablecloth. Wisps of green smoke drifted slowly upwards from the dark puddle of spilled wine.

A chair screeched at the back of the hall and fell with a bang. Tom turned to see Jezrin fleeing from the room.

"After him!" Tom cried. Taladon released Tom's arms and, together, Tom and his father raced after the traitorous wizard.

They burst from the palace into the courtyard to find Jezrin just ahead of them, making straight for Tempra's portal. Tom could see the disc of light getting smaller as it spun. *The portal's failing! I don't have long.*

He raced onwards, pushing his legs as fast as they would go. Taladon lengthened his stride. Even without his golden leg armour, he was the fastest runner in Avantia. He surged ahead of Tom and grabbed Jezrin's cloak, pulling him back from the portal.

Jezrin span, his face twisted with spite. He lifted his hand and sent a bolt of red light slamming into Taladon's chest. Taladon staggered back with a cry. Tom dived past and bundled into Jezrin, sending him tumbling. At the same moment, a bolt of lightning crackled down from above and struck the wizard, sparking around him, pinning him to the ground. Tom looked up to see Aduro leaning from a tower window.

Aduro lifted an eyebrow and smiled. "Well, I couldn't let him get away!" he said. "Young man, I don't know who you are, but the kingdom owes you thanks!"

Tom smiled, then took one last look
at his father's young face, now turned
up to Aduro as well. Tom's heart
clenched with a pang of longing.
I wish I could stay. But the portal
had dwindled almost to nothing. Tom

sprang towards it, and let the light swallow him.

Thud! He landed sprawling in the courtyard.

"Are you all right, Tom?" Captain Harkman asked, bending to kneel at his side, his face creased with concern. He held out a flagon of water. Tom rolled onto his back, and shook his head. His arms felt so weak, he didn't think he could hold the jug. He sat up slowly, met by a chorus of hearty chuckles from the soldiers on the chalk starting line.

"He must have worn himself out watching us!" Sully said, grinning. Tom glanced towards the table behind Captain Harkman, to see Elenna frowning at a sand-timer in her hand. She lifted the timer towards Tom, and smiled. The sand was running downwards. Just the way it should.

Tom pulled himself to his feet. "It was just a dizzy spell," he said. Looking around, he saw no sign of Tempra.

Captain Harkman clapped him hard on the back and laughed. "Must be all this sitting about – not good for a young lad like you. What you need is a nice Quest to sort you out."

Tom looked around the sunny courtyard, filled with smiling faces, then lifted his eyes to the palace, where flags bearing Hugo's coat of arms billowed in the breeze. It was one of the most ordinary sights

he'd seen, and it filled him with joy.
Everything's back to normal.

"You know,"Tom said, grinning
at Elenna, "this morning's been
strangely tiring. I think I'd quite like
a little break ..."

THE END

CONGRATULATIONS, YOU HAVE COMPLETED THIS QUEST!

At the end of each chapter you were awarded a special gold coin.
The QUEST in this book was worth an amazing 14 coins.

Look at the Beast Quest totem picture inside the back cover of this book to see how far you've come in your journey to become

MASTER OF THE BEASTS.

The more books you read, the more coins you will collect!

Do you want your own Beast Quest Totem?

1. Cut out and collect the coin below
2. Go to the Beast Quest website
3. Download and print out your totem
4. Add your coin to the totem
www.beastquest.co.uk/totem

Have you read the latest series of Beast Quest? Read on for a sneak peek at KRYTOR THE BLOOD BAT!

CHAPTER ONE

HOME!

"Ouch!" Elenna yelped, hopping onto one foot. "I've got a stone in my boot!"

Tom grinned as he watched his friend retrieve the stone and hurl it away.

"Just a little pebble," he said, pleased to have a moment to rest. "I can't believe you're complaining so much. We've been through worse."

"A lot worse." Elenna laughed. "Why couldn't Daltec magic us back from Gwildor?"

She has a point, Tom thought. The journey back to Avantia had been long and gruelling, taking them over both land and sea.

Tom lifted his chin. Being a Master of the Beasts meant doing difficult things. This journey home was just part of that. He pointed up ahead at the soaring towers of King Hugo's palace in the City. "Look, not that far now."

Read KRYTOR THE BLOOD BAT
to find out more!

FIGHT THE BEASTS,
FEAR THE MAGIC

Are you a BEAST QUEST mega fan?
Do you want to know about all the latest news,
competitions and books before anyone else?

Then join our Quest Club!

Visit the BEAST QUEST website
and sign up today!

www.beastquest.co.uk

CALLING ALL BEAST QUEST FANS - DRAW YOUR FAVOURITE BEAST!

Beast Quest is turning 10 next year and we want YOU to help us celebrate this special birthday. We're looking for drawings of your favourite Beasts to make into a special Beast Quest logo.

For each drawing we receive we will enter the artist into a special prize draw, where five lucky winners can win Beast Quest goodies!

To enter send your entries to:
Beast Quest Drawing Competition
Hachette Children's Books
Carmelite House
50 Victoria Embankment
London
EC47 0DZ

Closing date for entries 30th September 2016
For full terms and conditions please go to
www.hachettechildrensdigital.co.uk/terms/

31901059872368